Meet the Silver Hatch Gang

HarperCollins *Children's Books*

This is Roary the Racing Car.
He lives at Silver Hatch Race Track
with all of his friends.
Would you like to meet them?

This is Big Chris.

He looks after all of the cars at

Silver Hatch.

He also loves to sing!

Maxi is the fastest car
Roary has ever met.
He wins lots of races at Silver Hatch
but he is not always very nice
to the other cars.

Roary thinks it is more important to have friends than win races.

Cici is one of Roary's best friends.
She is a little pink stunt car
and loves to have fun!

3

This is Marsha the marshall.
She is in charge of all the races
and rides around on her scooter,
Zippee.

Zippee loves zipping around all day!

Drifter comes all the way from Japan
and has blue lights underneath.
Roary thinks he is the coolest car
at the race track.

Tin Top is an American stockcar.
He is covered in bumps
because he has been in so many races.

Tin Top is not a very careful driver!

Flash lives under the race track
and is always causing trouble!
He might be a little bit naughty
but Roary thinks that
Flash is one funny bunny.

Molecom helps Big Chris look after all of the cars in the pit lane.

Molecom can't see anything without his glasses!

Farmer Green lives on the farm.
Big Chris loves to get fresh eggs.

Farmer Green's truck, FB,
Delivers the eggs and milk
to the race track.

Big Chris lives at Silver Hatch in his caravan, Rusty.

Rusty likes to sleep
almost as much as
Big Chris likes to sing!

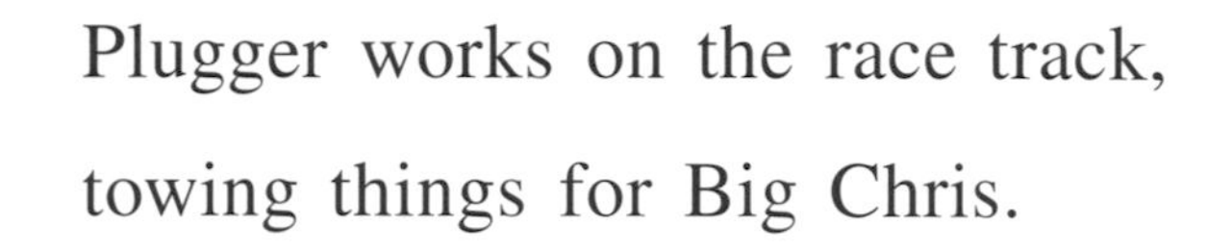

Plugger works on the race track,
towing things for Big Chris.

Dinkie lives in a field by the track
and loves to watch the races.
He is Roary's biggest fan.

This is Mr Carburettor.
He owns Silver Hatch race track
and all the cars.

He is very important and travels around his in helicopter, Hellie.

Now you have met
all of Roary's friends,
would you like to watch a race
at Silver Hatch one day?

88

Meet the Silver Hatch Gang

First published in the UK by HarperCollins Children's Books in 2008
HarperCollins Children's Books is a division of HarperCollins Publishers Ltd.

1 3 5 7 9 10 8 6 4 2

ISBN-13: 978-0-00-732232-9

www.roarytheracingcar.com

A CIP catalogue for this title is available from the British Library.

The HarperCollins website address is: www.harpercollins.co.uk

Printed and bound in China